The honey-flavoured
footprints led all
the way to the
food cupboard.

HUGLESS DOUGLAS

AND THE GREAT CAKE BAKE

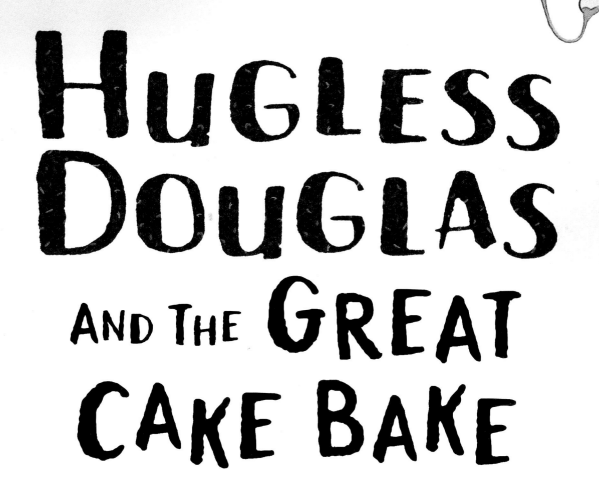

David Melling

Hodder
Children's
Books

Early one morning Douglas

was surprised to find a trail of footprints
running across his bed. They were sticky
and they tasted of honey!

'Who's been walking on my bed?' asked Douglas.

'Where's my honey?' Douglas gasped. He looked at the food very carefully.

'I can't eat any of this without honey on top! And

I'M REALLY HUNGRY.'

Douglas quickly changed and followed the
honey trail outside.

'If only I could find a clue to help me,' he sighed.

Then Douglas twitched his nose.
'I know that smell…'

'Aaah, hello Douglas!' baaed the sheep.

'Why are you wearing my honey?' asked Douglas.

'We're collecting everything we need to bake honey cakes,' said Flossie. 'Can you help?'

'Ooh yes,' said Douglas. 'I love baking.'

The sheep had collected BERRIES,
NUTS, CARROTS AND HONEY.

'Right then,' said Flossie. 'We need to put on our aprons and wash our paws.

Now let's bake!'

Flossie shouted instructions from her
recipe book and they set to work.

'I've finished! Can I eat some now?' asked Douglas.
'Not yet, it needs baking first,' said Flossie. 'But
if you're hungry, why not try these berries?'

'No thanks,' said Douglas.
'They haven't got honey on them. I'll wait.'

Douglas' tummy grumbled as he watched the sheep put dollops of the mixture onto baking trays and into the oven.

By now, everyone was **very** hungry.
Douglas found a plate and joined the
back of a bad-tempered queue.
There was pushing and nudging.

Then someone threw a carrot…

B-DoINK!

FOOD

FIGHT!

PING! went the oven.

'The cakes are ready!' said Flossie.

'Yay!' cried the sheep and they scrambled towards the delicious smell.

'Save some for me!' called Douglas.

But the sheep didn't hear and soon every single cake had been eaten.

'What am I going to eat now?' said Douglas, clutching his hungry tummy. He looked at the carrots on the floor and sighed.

He bit into one. 'Oh,' he said, a little surprised.
'That's nice!' Douglas wasn't used to eating
anything without honey on top.

He took a mouthful of berries. Even nicer!
And nuts… **'YUMMY!'** he cried.

'Carrots, berries and nuts are ALMOST as good as honey,' said Douglas.

'But not quite. Nothing beats

HONEY
AND
HUGS!'

HOW TO DECORATE CUPCAKE SHEEP...

1. Let your cakes cool.

3. Roll out the icing.

5. Add eyes, nose and ears.

How to Make Honey Cakes

You Will Need...

For the Cakes:
12-hole fairy cake tin

12 cupcake paper cases

115g softened butter

115g self-raising flour

115g caster sugar

2 eggs

1 tablespoon of honey

For the Icing:
50g melted butter

400g icing sugar

3 tablespoons cold water

2 tablespoons vanilla essence

1. Ask a grown-up to turn on the oven to 190°C/170°C fan/gas mark 5

2. MIX all the ingredients together really well in a bowl

3. Put 12 cupcake paper cases into a fairy cake tin and SPOON the mixture evenly between the cases

4. BAKE for 15 minutes or until the cakes are golden brown on top

5. Ask a grown-up to take the cakes out of the oven and place them on a wire rack to cool

6. When the cakes are cool, WHISK the ingredients for the icing together and SPREAD onto the cakes

7. EAT as quickly as possible